Zip

Written by Daniela Mora Chavarría

Illustrated by Andrea Altamirano

Collins

a torch for light

a hood

a torch for light

a hood

hook on the cord

red fur

hook on the cord

red fur

long tails

a wet foot

11

long tails

a wet foot

14

Review: After reading

Use your assessment from hearing the children read to choose any GPCs, words or tricky words that need additional practice.

Read 1: Decoding

- Use grapheme cards to make any words you need to practise. Model reading those words, using teacher-led blending.
- Ask the children to follow as you read the whole book, demonstrating fluency and prosody.

Read 2: Vocabulary

- Look back through the book and discuss the pictures. Encourage the children to talk about details that stand out for them. Use a dialogic talk model to expand on their ideas and recast them in full sentences as naturally as possible.
- Work together to expand vocabulary by naming objects in the pictures that children do not know.
- On page 6, ask the children to point to the words that tell you where the hook is. (**on the cord**) Discuss what sort of cord it is, referring to the title of the book if necessary. (*a zip wire*)

Read 3: Comprehension

- Talk about zip wires and adventure playground equipment. Ask the children to describe adventure playground equipment they have been on or would like to try, and why.
- Reread pages 2 and 3. Discuss what the text tells us about the setting. Ask: How do we know that it is dark? (e.g. *they need **a torch for light***) How do we know it isn't dry? (e.g. *the girl is wearing **a hood***)
- Turn to pages 14 and 15. Encourage the children to retell and describe the events in sequence. Can they think of a label for each of the small pictures? (e.g. *a torch for light*)